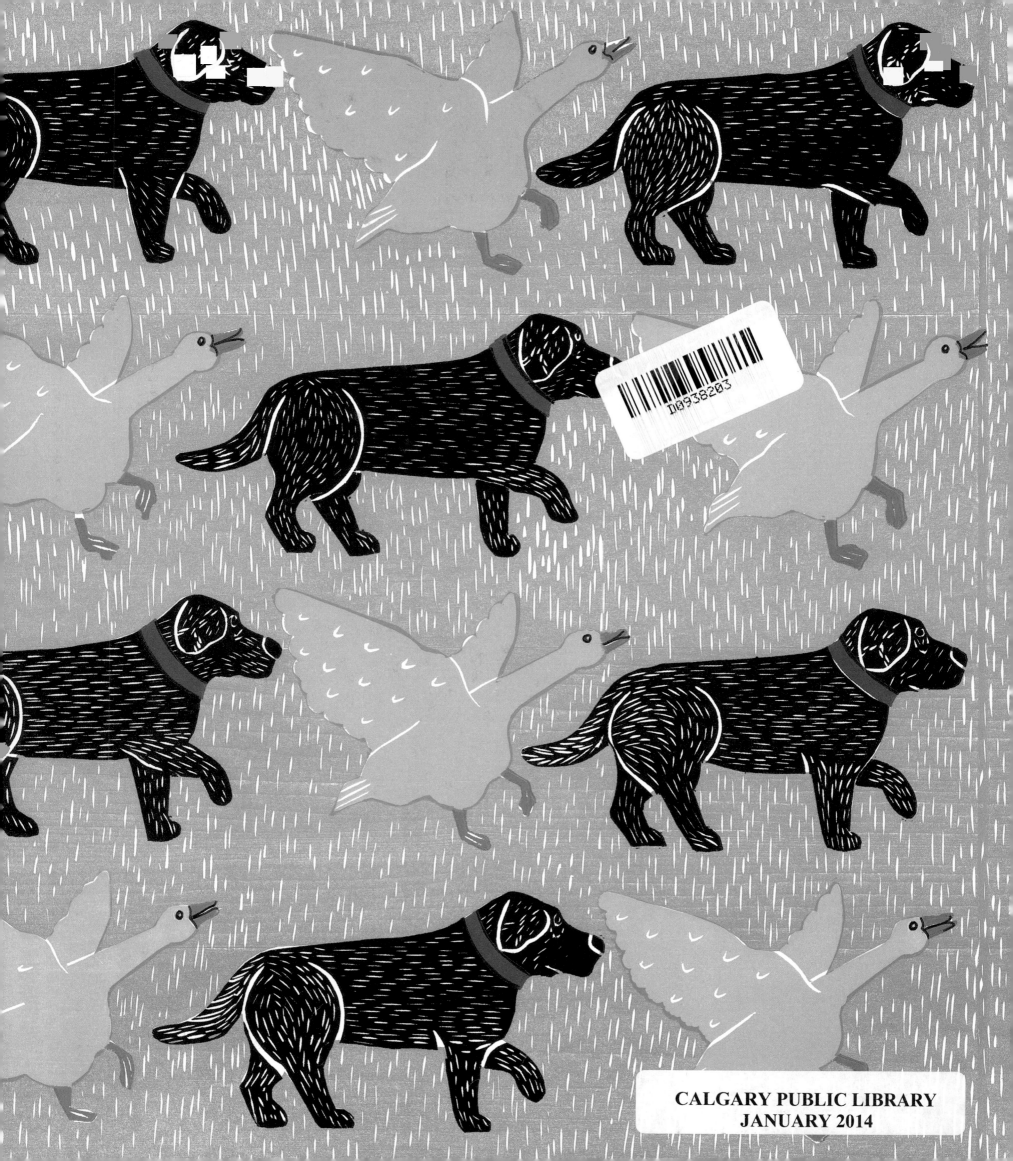

Also by Stephen Huneck:

Sally Gets a Job
Sally Goes to the Beach
Sally Goes to the Farm
Sally Goes to the Mountains
Sally Goes to the Vet
Sally's Great Balloon Adventure
Sally's Snow Adventure
The Dog Chapel

Sally Goes
to the Farm

Written and Illustrated by
Stephen Huneck

Abrams Books for Young Readers
New York

Acknowledgments

I wish to thank Howard Reeves and Emily Farbman for their enthusiasm. I wish to thank Chantel Amey and Mike Lamp for all their help in the studio. My thanks to Will Seippel and Joel Gotler for their friendship. And a special thanks to my wonderful wife Gwen.

Artist's Note

To create a woodcut print, I first draw the design of the future print in crayon, laying out the prospective shapes and colors. I then carve one block of wood for each color in the appropriate shape. The result is a series of carved blocks, one for each color in the print. After a block has been inked with its respective color, acid-free archival paper is laid onto the block and hand rubbed. I repeat the process for each color block. When this process is completed, I hang the prints to dry. —S.H.

You may visit Stephen Huneck's website at: www.huneck.com.
Original font design by Stephen Huneck
The artwork for each picture is prepared with woodblock prints on paper.
The text is set in 24-point Huneck Regular.

Designer: Edward Miller

Library of Congress Cataloging-in-Publication Data
Huneck, Stephen.
Sally goes to the farm / written and illustrated by Stephen Huneck.
p. cm.
SUMMARY: Sally, a black Labrador retriever, goes to a farm where she enjoys various activities.
ISBN 978-0-8109-4498-5
1. Dogs—Fiction. 2. Labrador retriever—Fiction. 3. Farm
life—Fiction. 4. Domestic animals—Fiction. I. Title.
PZ7.H8995 San 2002
[E]—dc21
2001003750

Printed in China
15 14 13 12 11 10 9 8

Abrams Books for Young Readers are available at special discounts when purchased in quantity for premiums and promotions as well as fundraising or educational use. Special editions can also be created to specification. For details, contact specialmarkets@abramsbooks.com or the address below.

THE ART OF BOOKS SINCE 1949
115 West 18th Street
New York, NY 10011
www.abramsbooks.com

Sally Goes to the Farm

To America's farmers
and their faithful dogs.

"Sally, we are going to the farm.
There is someone I want you to meet.
Her name is Molly."

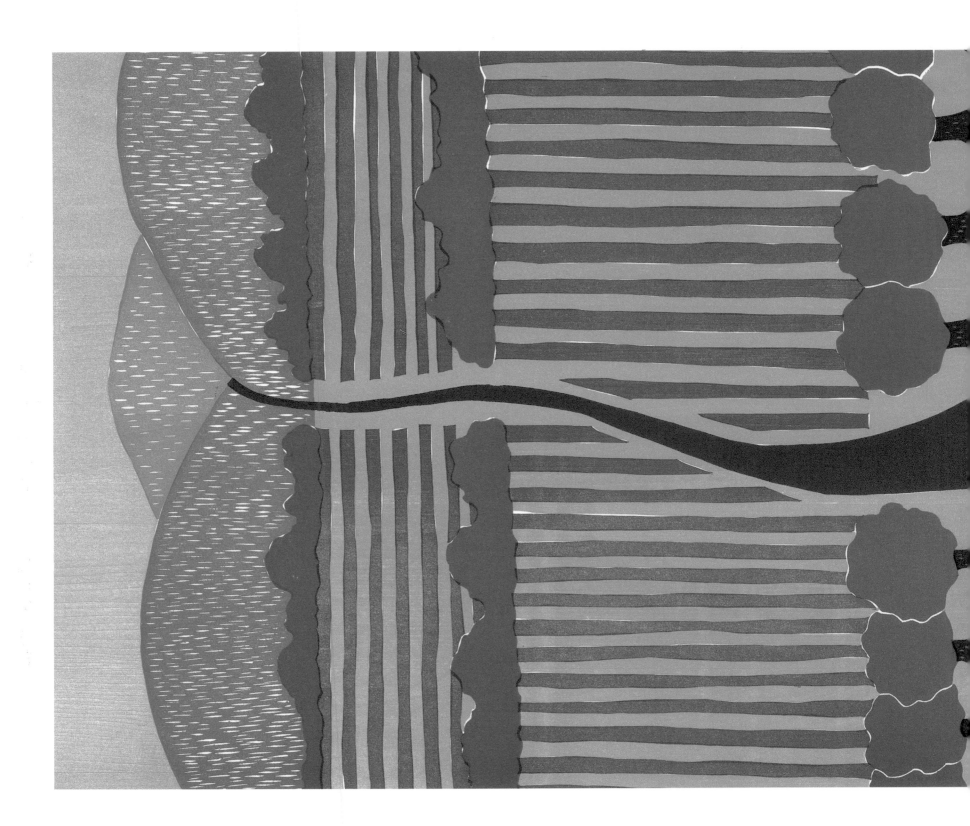

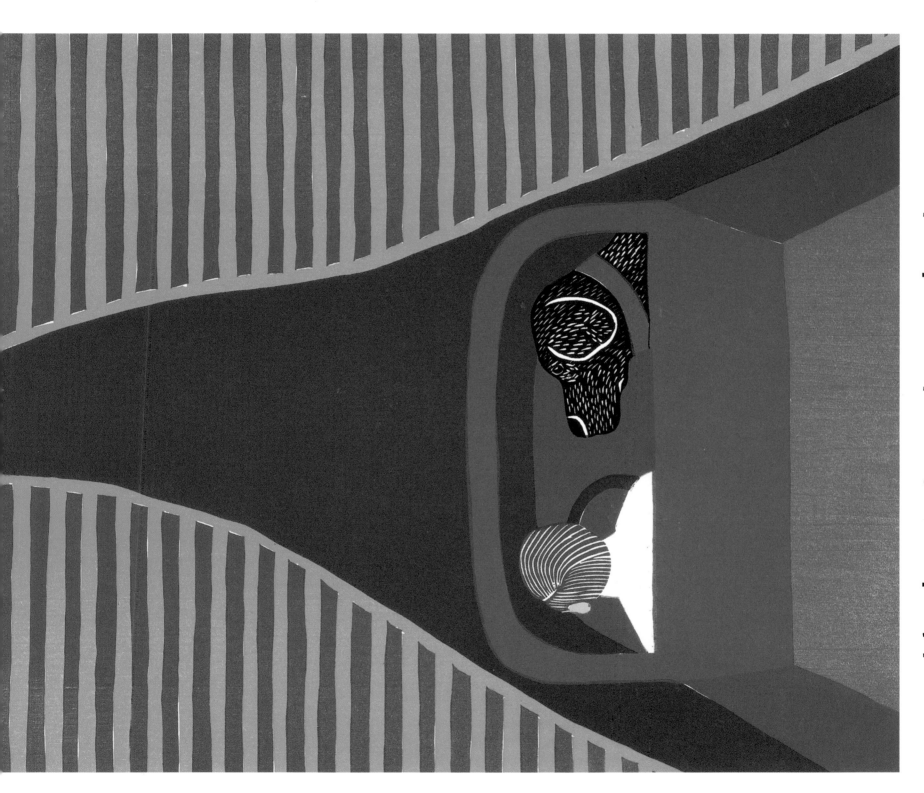

We drive for miles and miles.

We see the farm

and smell it, too.

We say our hellos.

Hello, Molly.

Hello, Sally.

Come on, Sally.
There is someone I want you to meet.

Her name is Bessie.
She has a treat.

Fresh milk!

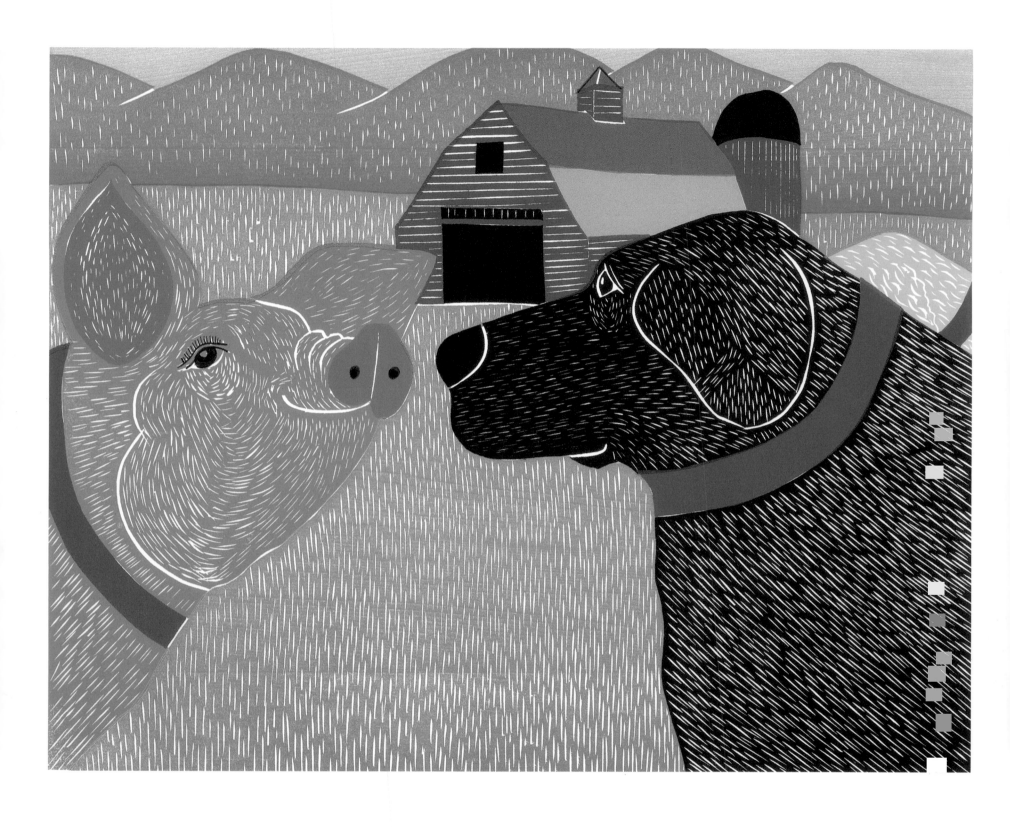

Hi, my name is Penelope.
Would you like some lunch?

We eat like pigs.

Sally, meet Harriet.
She loves to horse around.

We play some tug-of-war.

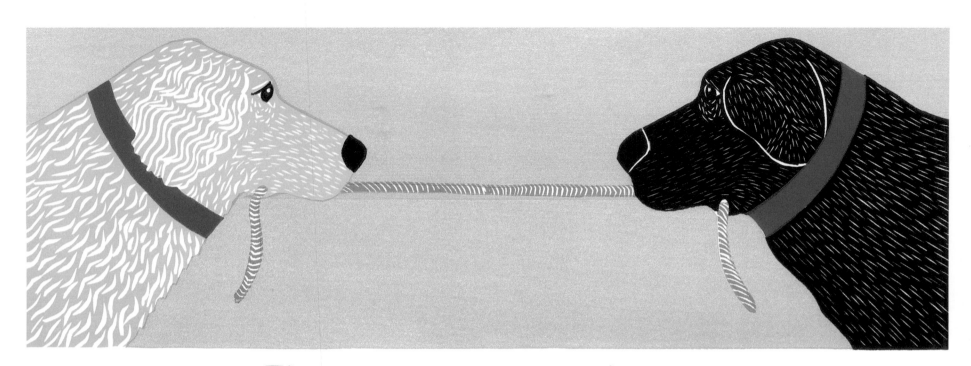

This game is so much fun,

we do not care who wins.

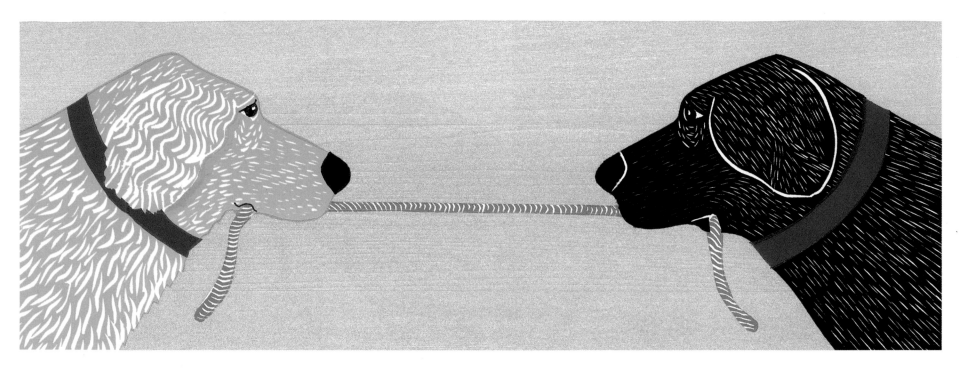

We help the farmer plow his fields.

We meet the scarecrow. He seems nice.

But he does not say a word.

Run, Sally, run,

or we will get a goosing!

Quick, let's go inside.

What lucky dogs we are!

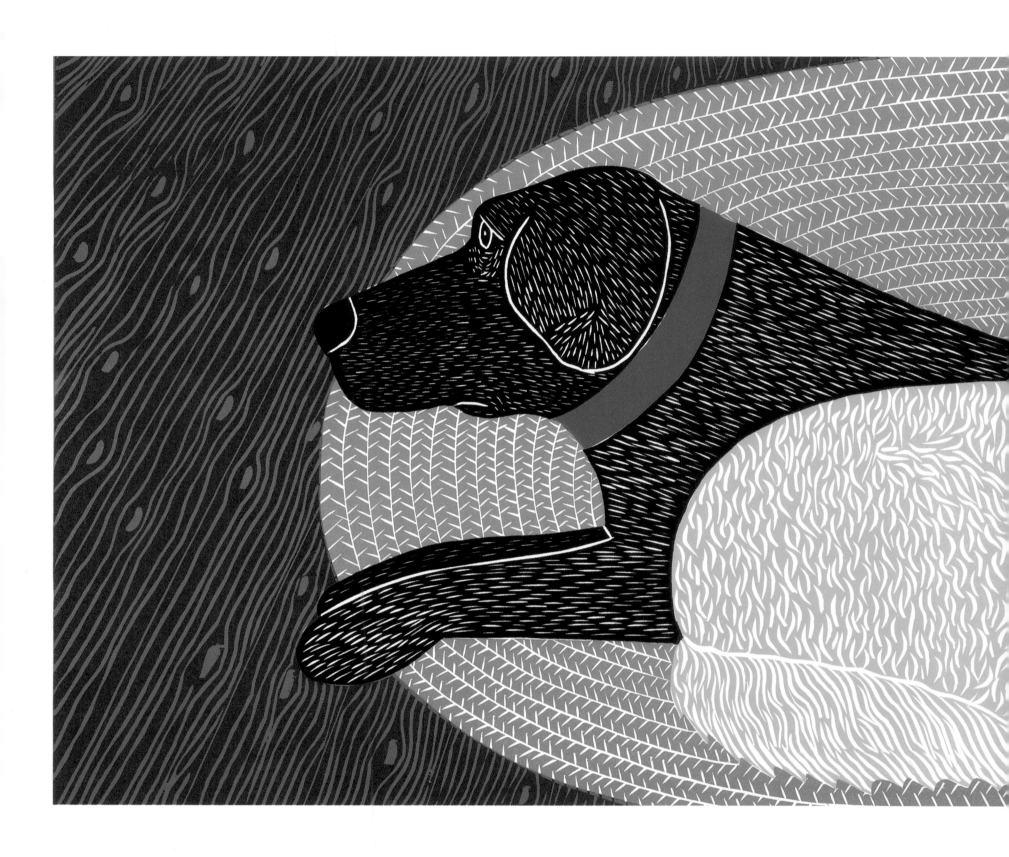

We wolf down the pie,

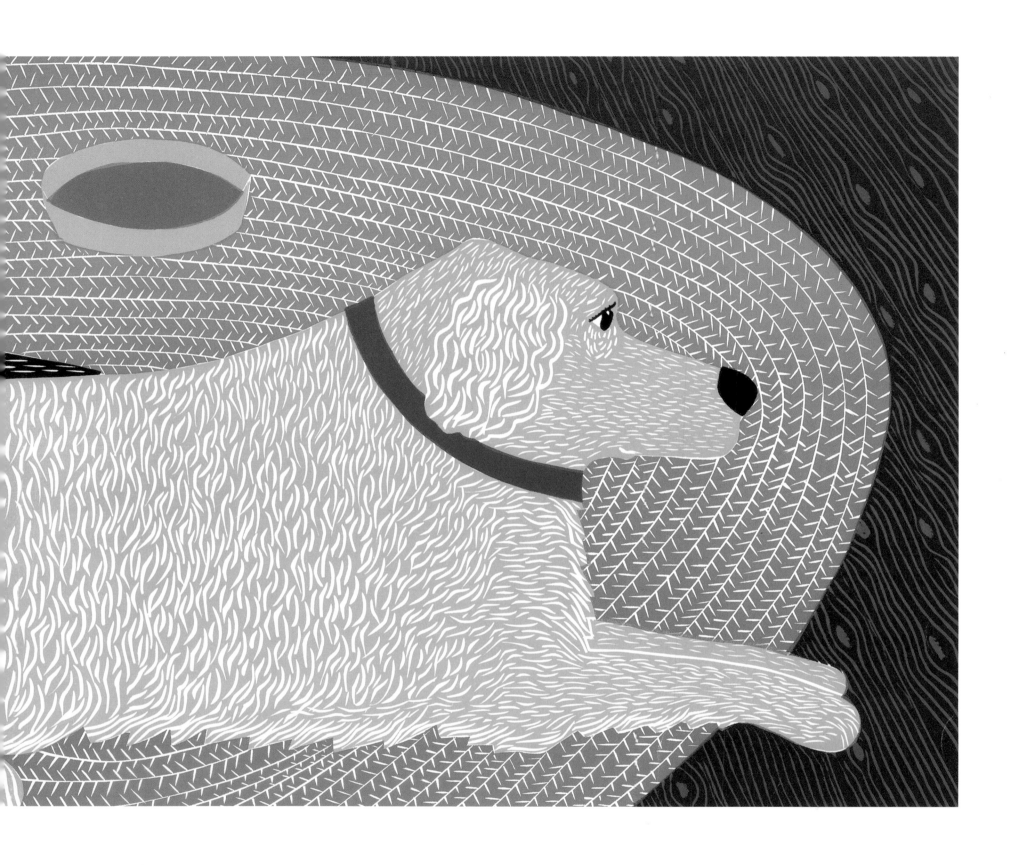

then take a well-earned rest.

Farming is hard work.

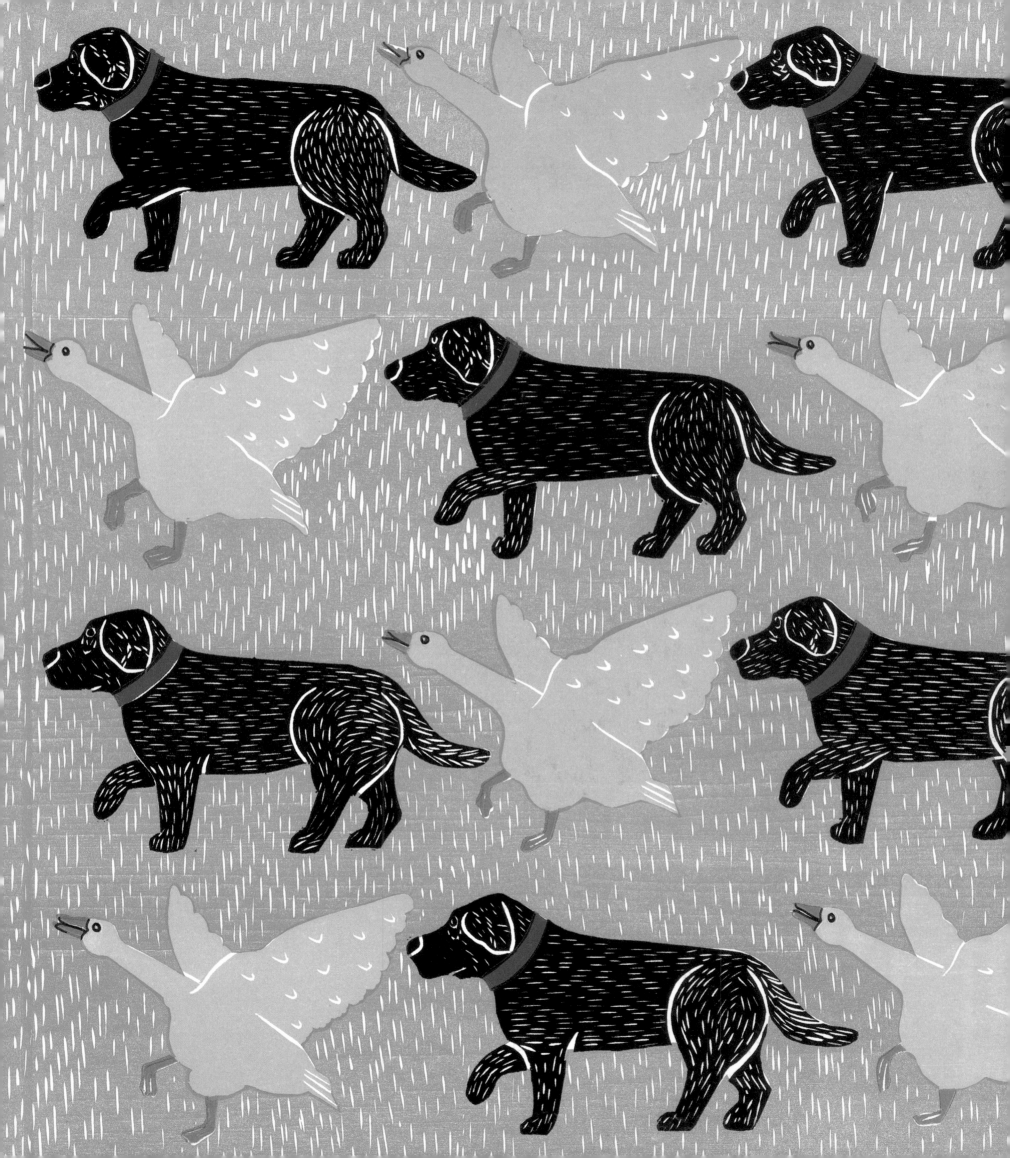